$5.65
B+T
3-12-82

BASKETBALL
is for me

BASKETBALL
is for me

Lowell A. Dickmeyer

photographs by
Alan Oddie

 Lerner Publications Company Minneapolis

The author wishes to thank the faculty and staff of Banyan Elementary School, Newbury Park, California, Mr. and Mrs. Clifford Severn and Catherine, and the Minnesota Fillies.

All photographs by Alan Oddie except for the following: page 33, Doug Mazzapica; pages 34, 35, Ken Papaceo; pages 40, 41, David Grupa, Spectrum Images.

LIBRARY OF CONGRESS CATALOGING IN PUBLICATION DATA

Dickmeyer, Lowell A.
Basketball is for me.

(A Sports for Me Book)
SUMMARY: Jenny and her classmates learn how to dribble, pass, shoot and rebound as they prepare for their first game.

1. Basketball—Juvenile literature. [1. Basketball] I. Oddie, Alan. II. Title. III. Series.

GV885.1.D52   796.32'32   79-16954
ISBN 0-8225-1089-8

Manufactured in the United States of America.
Published simultaneously in Canada by J. M. Dent & Sons (Canada) Ltd., Don Mills, Ontario.

International Standard Book Number: 0-8225-1089-8
Library of Congress Catalog Card Number: 79-16954

2 3 4 5 6 7 8 9 10 85 84 83 82 81

Hi! My name is Jenny. I'm in the fourth grade at Banyan School. In gym class, we are playing basketball. I really enjoy this sport.

My older sister Lana also likes to play basketball. Lana played on a woman's team when she was at college. Sometimes Lana and I practice together.

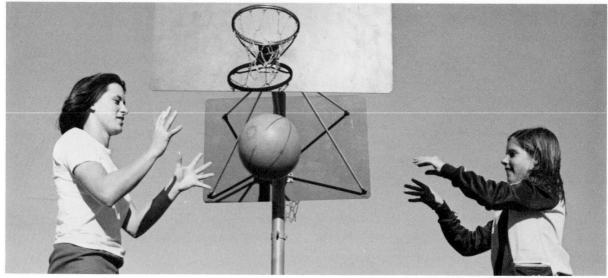

In basketball, two teams try to score points by putting a ball through a hoop or basket. Each team has five players. When your team has the ball, you are the **offense**. The offense tries to score points. When your opponents have the ball, you become the **defense**. The defense tries to get the ball back and prevent the other team from scoring.

7

During play, if the ball goes through the basket successfully, you score two points. A **free throw** is worth only one point. A free throw is a chance to make a basket without defensive players guarding you. You are awarded one or two free throws if an opponent pushes or trips you during play.

I learned these and other things about basketball in gym class. Every day after math class, I would hurry to the locker room to change into my gym clothes. All you need to play basketball are a shirt, shorts, socks, and gym shoes. The only other equipment is the ball and two baskets with backboards.

We started each gym class with some exercises. We did push-ups, sit-ups, and jumping jacks. Because jumping is so important in basketball, we did heel raisers, too. These strengthened our legs and ankles.

We worked hard on running, too, because you do so much running in basketball games. We jogged around the gym. Then we practiced **sprinting**, or running very fast for short distances.

After exercising, our class began practicing basketball skills. Basketball players can move the ball by **dribbling** or passing it. Dribbling means to bounce the ball off the floor using either hand. You cannot use both hands at the same time to dribble.

As long as you keep dribbling, you can move up or down the **court**, or playing field. But once you stop dribbling, you can move only one step. The other foot must stay in place on the floor. This foot is called your **pivot foot**. If you take more than one step while holding the ball, you will be **traveling**.

Traveling is against the rules, and you will have to give the ball to your opponents.

You are allowed to dribble continuously only once each time you have the ball. Once you stop dribbling, you will have to pass the ball or shoot. It is usually best to keep the ball moving, so get rid of it as soon as you stop dribbling.

Ms. Abney, our gym teacher, said that we had to be able to dribble well with either hand. Good basketball players can also change directions while dribbling. We practiced these skills by dribbling in and out of a line of chairs. Ms. Abney reminded us to always keep our heads up while dribbling.

During games, you should try to keep your body between the ball and your opponent. If you are closely guarded, keep your dribble low. These things make it more difficult for your opponent to steal the ball.

Passing is a faster method of moving the basketball. There are several ways to pass the ball. The first pass we practiced was the **two-handed chest pass**.

You throw a chest pass from chest height. As you throw, step forward and straighten your arms. Your fingers should point at the **pass receiver.** This is the person to whom you are throwing the ball. The ball should reach your teammate at chest height, too.

The **overhead pass** is similar to the chest pass except that the ball is thrown from over the head. Like all passes, the overhead pass should be thrown smoothly and on target. A pass is no good if it is too hard to handle by your teammate.

Another two-handed pass is the **bounce pass**. The pass starts like the chest pass, but you throw the ball down so that it hits the floor before bouncing up to your teammate. This is a hard pass for your opponents to steal.

The **baseball pass** and **hook pass** are one-handed passes. The ball is thrown over the shoulder for both of these passes. Your throwing arm is bent back for the baseball pass. You keep your arm straight with the hook pass.

Pass receiving is just as important as throwing a pass. To be a good receiver, you must always be moving to stay "open." This means that you should get in front of any defensive player who could possibly block a pass. You should always keep your eyes on the ball and step forward to meet the pass.

Shooting baskets is another important offensive skill. Ms. Abney taught us the **one-handed set shot** and the **lay-up**.

The one-handed set shot is a good shot if you are left unguarded for a moment. It is an accurate shot at short or long distances.

To prepare for the set shot, hold the ball with both hands at chin level. Spread your fingers behind the ball. One foot should be slightly in front of the other, and your knees should be bent. Aim at a spot just over the rim of the basket, or at a point on the backboard so the ball can bounce into the basket.

The set shot is usually used when shooting free throws. The player must stand behind the free-throw line. You should practice so that you can make most free throws. They are an important way to increase your team's score.

The lay-up shot is always made near the basket. The shot is taken after a short, two-step running approach. To practice this shot, we lined up a short distance away from the basket. Then we ran up for our lay-up shots.

To make a lay-up shot, take a step toward the basket. As you take your next step up in the air, carry the ball toward the basket with both hands. When you reach your highest point, your outside hand should guide the ball into the basket.

Not all of your shots will go into the basket. Most unsuccessful shots **rebound**, or bounce off the rim or backboard. Catching rebounds is a very important offensive and defensive skill. It helps to always be prepared by keeping your arms up.

Defensive skills include guarding your opponents. When you are in a good guarding stance, hold one hand high to stop the pass and one hand low to possibly interfere with the dribble.

When guarding, always stay between your opponent and the basket. Stay back far enough so that your opponent can't quickly move around you. Use a shuffle or sliding motion to move right or left to block your opponent's movements.

Blocking shots is another job for the defense. If you cannot actually slap the ball out of its path to the basket, you should keep your hand near your opponent's face so that the shooter cannot see the basket.

You must be careful, however, not to hold, trip, push, or run into the player you are guarding. If you do, you will be charged with a **foul**. The player you have fouled is awarded a free throw. When you have committed five fouls, you can no longer play in the game.

Every day in gym class, we practiced our basketball skills. We dribbled, passed, and shot baskets and free throws. We practiced rebounding and guarding. Ms. Abney promised us that we would start playing actual games in a few days.

I was excited about playing a real game soon. My sister Lana was happy for me, too.

She told me that she had a surprise for me. She had tickets for the men's basketball game at her college. And she wanted to take me to see the game.

It was so exciting to watch a basketball game. The men were so tall that they seemed to just lay the ball in the basket.

Lana told me to pay close attention to the defense. Sometimes they played **person-to-person.** This means that each player guarded one special player on the opposing team. Other times the team was in a **zone** defense. This means that players guarded any opponents who came into their section of the court.

We played person-to-person defense when my gym class played its first game. The class was divided into five-player teams. The teams took turns playing 10-minute games.

Each player on the teams has a special job to do. Two of the players are **guards**. They usually play at the points farthest from the basket. When their team misses a shot at the basket, the guards quickly switch to playing defense.

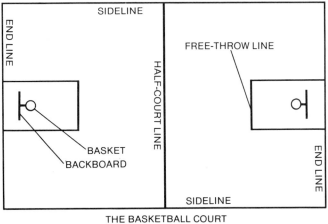

THE BASKETBALL COURT

One player on each team is the **center**. The center plays in the area closest to the basket. The center is usually the tallest player on the team. This person should be a good shooter and rebounder.

The other two players on the team are the **forwards**. Forwards should also be good shooters and rebounders. They usually play near the corners of the court on either side of the basket.

All the players on a team should help to keep the ball moving until one person is open for a shot.

One day in class, Ms. Abney said we would play a night game. We could invite our families to come and watch us play. I couldn't wait to tell Lana and my parents.

When I got home, Lana had some good news, too. She had received a letter from the Minnesota Fillies inviting her to try out for

their team. The Fillies are a professional women's basketball team. The Fillies had sent some tickets for their next game so Lana could watch them play.

Lana and I went to the Fillies game together. We cheered every time the Fillies made a good play. The action was fast and exciting.

After the game, Lana and I had some ice cream. We talked about basketball and my upcoming game. I couldn't wait to play.

The night of our game, the class divided into a red team and a blue team. I was a forward on the blue team.

The game started with a **jump ball**. For a jump ball, the referee tosses the ball in the air between two opposing players. Each player tries to tap the ball to a teammate standing nearby.

The red team got the ball, so our team quickly went into its person-to-person defense. Our opponents scored. Now the blue team had the ball. I had a chance to score, so I shot.

Bill was guarding me, and he hit my hand. The referee blew his whistle and called a foul. I got two free throws because I was fouled while I was shooting.

I made my first free throw and missed the second. Everybody jumped for the rebound.

I was having fun. Both teams scored many points. We all had a chance to practice our basketball skills. I knew Lana was cheering for me. I was on my way to becoming a basketball player just like her.

Words about BASKETBALL

BACKBOARD: The large flat surface to which the basket is attached

CENTER: The player, usually the tallest team member, who is positioned close to the basket. This person directs play, shoots, and jumps for rebounds.

CHARGING: A foul caused by an offensive player running into an opponent

DEFENSE: The team that does not have possession of the ball. Their job is to stop the other team from scoring.

DOUBLE DRIBBLE: A rule violation that occurs when a player who has stopped dribbling starts to dribble a second time. The player must turn the ball over to the other team.

DRIBBLE: To bounce the ball with one hand while running or standing still

FORWARDS: The two offensive players who usually play on the sides of the court. They should be good shooters and rebounders.

FOUL: An illegal play by players who hold, push, trip, or run into an opponent

FOUL OUT: To become disqualified from the game after committing five fouls

FREE-THROW LINE: A line 15 feet from the basket behind which an unguarded player shoots

GUARDS: The two players who usually play in the back court. These players should be fast runners, good dribblers, and quick to take up defensive positions.

JUMP BALL: The play that starts the game and the second half. The referee throws the ball up between two opposing players who jump and attempt to tap the ball to their teammates. A jump ball is also called when two opposing players hold onto the ball at the same time during play.

LAY-UP: A shot taken very close to the basket after a short running approach

OFFENSE: The team in possession of the ball

PERSON-TO-PERSON DEFENSE: A defensive formation in which each player is assigned to guard one opposing player

PIVOT FOOT: The foot you hold stationary on the floor after you stop dribbling. You are allowed to step in any direction with your other foot.

REBOUND: To catch a ball that bounces off the rim or backboard after a shot

TRAVELING: A rule violation that occurs when a player in possession of the ball takes more than one step without dribbling

ZONE DEFENSE: A defensive formation in which players are assigned to guard a particular section of the court

ABOUT THE AUTHOR

LOWELL A. DICKMEYER is active in athletics as a participant, instructor, and writer. He is particularly interested in youth sport programs, and each summer he organizes sports camps for hundreds of youngsters. Mr. Dickmeyer has been a college physical education instructor and an elementary school principal in southern California.

ABOUT THE PHOTOGRAPHER

ALAN ODDIE was born and raised in Scotland. He now resides in Santa Monica, California. In addition to his work as a photographer, Mr. Oddie is an author and a producer of educational filmstrips. He is currently the staff photographer for *Franciscan Communications*.